The LEGENDS of KING ARTHUR

MERLIN, MAGIC AND DRAGONS

CB007103

Dados Internacionais de Catalogação na Publicação (CIP) de acordo com ISBD

M469t   Mayhew, Tracey
           Twelve rebel kings / adaptado por Tracey Mayhew. – Jandira : W. Books, 2025.
           96 p. ; 12,8cm x 19,8cm. – (The legends of king Arthur)

           ISBN: 978-65-5294-165-7

           1. Literatura infantojuvenil. 2. Literatura Infantil. 3. Clássicos. 4. Literatura inglesa. 5. Lendas. 6. Folclore. 7. Mágica. 8. Cultura Popular. I. Título. II. Série.

2025-618   CDD 028.5
                                              CDU 82-93

Elaborado por Vagner Rodolfo da Silva - CRB-8/9410
Índice para catálogo sistemático:
1. Literatura infantojuvenil 028.5
2. Literatura infantojuvenil 82-93

The Legends of King Arthur: Merlin, Magic, and Dragons
Text © Sweet Cherry Publishing Limited, 2020
Inside illustrations © Sweet Cherry Publishing Limited, 2020
Cover illustrations © Sweet Cherry Publishing Limited, 2020

Text by Tracey Mayhew
Illustrations by Mike Phillips

© 2025 edition:
Ciranda Cultural Editora e Distribuidora Ltda.

1st edition in 2025
www.cirandacultural.com.br

THE LEGENDS OF KING ARTHUR

TWELVE REBEL KINGS

Retold by
Tracey Mayhew

Illustrated by
Mike Phillips

W. Books

Chapter One

Arthur Pendragon had been king for four years. He had done a lot to make Britain safer: he had defeated warlords, settled feuds, and made sure that all in his kingdom were well cared for.

Seeing his successes, many other kings had pledged their loyalty, acknowledging Arthur as High King – but not all.

Lot, King of Lothian, in Scotland, thought that he would make a far better King of Britain than Arthur. He already had the support of ten other kings on his side. Lot sent word to Camelot that he and his men wanted to meet in battle to decide, once and for all, who should rule. Arthur accepted the challenge.

As his army marched, Arthur sent scouts ahead. When reports came back that Lot and his men were only three days' ride away, Arthur told his men to set up camp on the edge of Bedegraine Forest to await them. That way when the two armies met, Arthur's would be rested, whilst King Lot's would be tired from the journey. In the meantime, Arthur and his men would practise their swordplay.

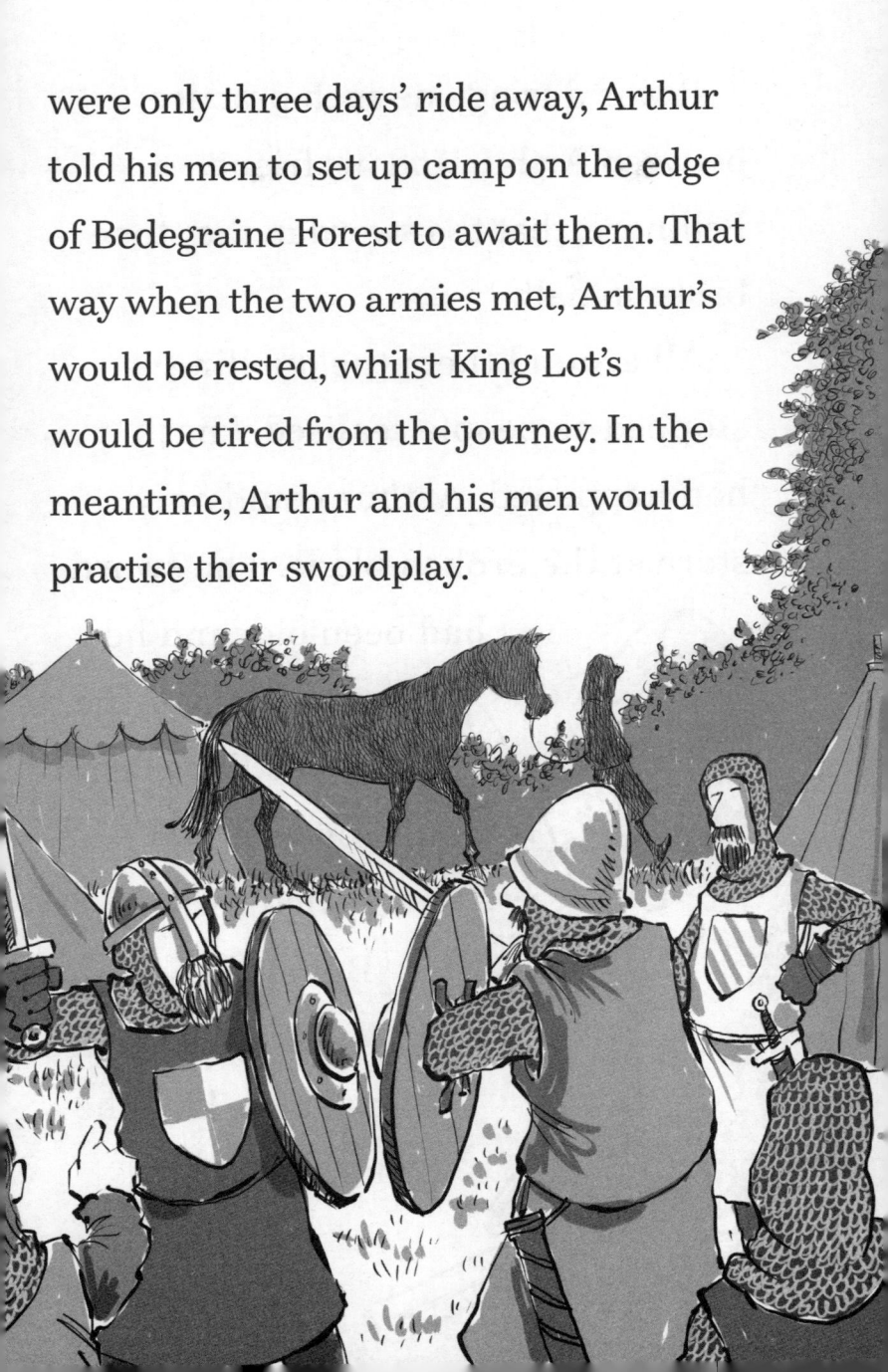

It was during one such practice, between Arthur and his friend Pellinore, that the sword in the stone broke in half.

All around them the duelling stopped as people realised what had happened. Arthur could only stare at the broken blade. The sword had been old, and he was no longer the scared little farm boy who had pulled it free. But still …

'This sword made me king,' he murmured.

'Your Majesty, forgive me,' Pellinore begged, looking horrified. 'I never–'

'Stop!' Arthur interrupted. 'It is better it happen now, amongst friends, than when we face the enemy in battle.' He retrieved the broken piece from the grass. 'But I will need another sword.'

Even as he said it, Arthur could not imagine anything replacing the famous sword in the stone.

'Perhaps I can help?'

They turned as Merlin approached.

In the years since Arthur had become king, Merlin had hardly changed. Arthur, however, looked completely different. His blonde hair was longer, and he had grown a beard that he kept neatly trimmed. Years of weapons drills and wearing armour had given him muscles he never had as a boy.

'I have seen a sword in my dreams,' Merlin continued. 'A sword so great, it will drive fear into the hearts of your enemies.'

Arthur's brother Kay raised his eyebrows. 'Sounds like a sword worthy of a king. Where is it?'

'A day's ride from here.'

Arthur was incredulous. '*A day's ride?* Merlin, I am about to lead my men into battle. I cannot abandon them for a whole day!' He shook his head. 'We have swords here. I'll use one of those.'

'Your Majesty, you don't understand–'

'I understand that it has taken too long to win these men's trust for me to leave them on the brink of battle to fetch a sword.'

'Sire, this is not just any sword. It is *Excalibur*.'

Arthur and the others stared blankly.

'It was made in Avalon,' Merlin added.

That piqued Arthur's interest. 'Your homeland?'

'Indeed.'

'So it's a magic sword?' Kay asked.

Merlin smiled. 'Not quite. But there is no other sword like it in the whole of Britain. With Excalibur in your hand, Sire, you will never need another weapon.'

'I suppose if one sword can win me a crown, another might help me to keep it,' Arthur mused. 'How do we find this *Excalibur*?'

'There is a lake not far from here. The Lady of the Lake awaits us there.'

Arthur looked surprised. 'She knows we're coming?'

'Yes, Your Majesty.'

Arthur turned to Kay. 'Will you take charge whilst I'm gone?'

'It would be my honour.'

'Well, Merlin,' Arthur declared, 'let's not keep your lady waiting.'

Chapter Two

Arthur galloped across the open plain, enjoying the feeling of freedom. Thanks to his latest campaign, it had been a long while since he had let Llamrei, his black mare, run freely. Llamrei, it seemed, was just as keen to escape the camp as he was.

But Arthur knew they had to return
as soon as they could. King Lot's forces
were less than two days away now.

'Are we almost there?' Arthur called,
as he slowed to let Merlin catch up.

'The lake is just beyond that hill.'

As they reached the top of the hill, Arthur
reined Llamrei to a stop beside Merlin.
Below, the lake stretched out before them,
its surface as smooth and clear as a looking
glass. Hidden from the rest of the world,
it was silent and peaceful.

But there was no woman
in sight.

'Where is the lady you spoke of, Merlin?' Arthur asked, feeling his horse begin to fidget.

'She is here.'

Confused, Arthur nudged Llamrei forwards, following Merlin's steed down the hill to the shore. Dismounting, Arthur tied the reins to a nearby tree. He kept scanning the banks. 'I don't see anyone.'

Saying nothing, Merlin walked to the lake's edge. He bent down and dipped his fingers into the water, sending ripples across its surface.

Arthur sighed impatiently. 'Merlin, I–' But he fell silent when the water took on a golden light.

Arthur could only stare in wonder as the glow seemed to concentrate in the centre of the lake, where the water began swirling and rising into the air. Gradually, it

took on the shape of a woman.

'Wh-who–?' Arthur spluttered, pointing a shaking finger.

'She is the Lady of the Lake,' Merlin replied, smiling.

Arthur was captivated. The lady was beautiful. She had golden hair that fell around her shoulders and a white dress that shone in the sun. She smiled radiantly at Arthur and began moving gracefully towards him.

'How is she walking on water?' Arthur gasped.

Rather than answer, Merlin laid a hand on Arthur's back and urged him forwards. Unable to resist the silent command, or

the woman's beauty, Arthur stepped
into the lake. He met the lady partway,
where the water reached his thighs.

We meet at last, Arthur Pendragon.
Her soft voice echoed inside his head.
Her lips had not moved.

'My lady,' Arthur
replied, bowing his

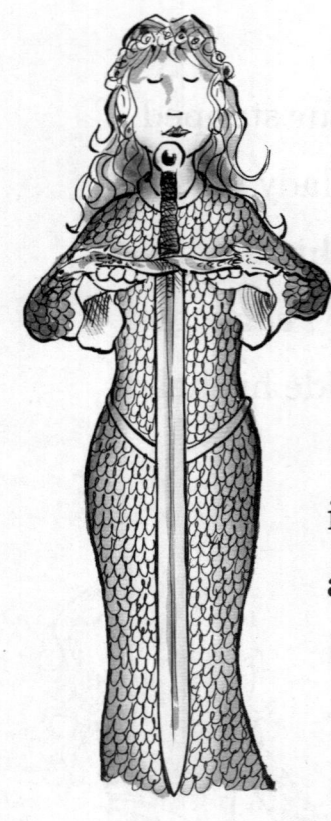

head. His eyes landed on the sword in her hands. The cross guard was gold and the pommel had a blood-red stone at its centre. The blade alone was longer than his old sword had been, and it seemed to hold just as much light as it reflected. Droplets of water slid down it in slow motion. Arthur tore his gaze free.

The Lady of the Lake smiled at him.

Kneel.

Powerless to refuse, Arthur knelt, not

caring that the cool water now ringed his waist, or that the lady towered above him.

Arthur, I give you Excalibur. With it you will defeat those who stand against you and bring peace to the land.

Reaching out, Arthur took the sword and gazed in awe at the cross guard: two dragons entwined.

'It's beautiful,' he whispered.

It is not all that I have to give you. A

plain black leather scabbard
materialised in her hand.
*This scabbard is yet more
powerful than the sword.
With this at your side, your
enemies can harm but not kill
you. As long as you wear it,
you will be protected.*

Arthur took the scabbard reverently
and slid Excalibur inside.

'Thank you, my lady.'

*Now stand, Arthur. King Lot's men
draw near. Return to yours and lead
them to victory.*

Arthur stood and bowed deeply,
meeting her sapphire blue eyes as she
walked – no, *receded* backwards to the

middle of the lake. There she became a glow, then a swirl, and disappeared from view.

Arthur turned to the shore, hastily buckling the scabbard around his waist. 'We must leave, Merlin. There's no time to lose.'

Chapter Three

The journey back seemed to take far longer than the outward one. Arthur and Merlin reached camp just as the sun was setting, rousing triumphant cries from the men. Everyone was eager to see Excalibur and Arthur was happy to show it. He was proud to be the owner of such a magnificent sword, and he knew word would soon spread that he had it. What nobody asked about, and what Arthur did not mention, was the scabbard.

'Your Majesty!' Bedivere, one of Arthur's most trusted men, came running towards him. 'Scouts have just returned! Lot's forces are camped just two miles from here, on the other side of the forest.'

Arthur frowned. 'They have arrived sooner than I expected.' His gaze swept over his men. 'We ride out tonight,' he announced.

'Tonight, Majesty?' Kay asked, bewildered.

'If we leave tonight, we keep the element of surprise. Until our allies arrive, Lot's men outnumber us. Surprise is the greatest weapon we have.' He stepped away, raising his voice for every man to hear. 'Ready yourselves! We ride out soon!'

At this order, men scattered. They returned to their tents to put on their armour and collect their weapons.

Arthur turned to Merlin. 'Are you certain Ban and Bors are coming?' he asked. It had been days since the French kings' arrival in Britain, but Arthur had heard nothing since.

'They are not far,' Merlin assured him. 'I will ride out to meet them and lead them to you.'

Satisfied, Arthur he made his way to Llamrei. Stroking her nose, he whispered, 'This is it, girl.'

As if in response, the horse snorted, throwing her head back and whinnying.

Arthur smiled as he untied her from the tree and mounted her in one swift move. Cantering to the edge of camp, it wasn't long before his men were gathered before him.

'Tonight, we fight for Britain,' Arthur called, his voice showing no sign of the fear he still felt before every battle. 'Tomorrow, we celebrate our victory!'

A roar went up around him. Raising Excalibur, Arthur turned Llamrei and spurred her into a gallop. His army thundered behind him, the sound eventually drowning his fears. With his men on his side, not to mention an enchanted sword, King Lot didn't stand a chance!

Under cover of trees, Arthur watched
King Lot and his men laughing by their
campfires, enjoying a rest after another
long day in the saddle. All around
Arthur, his men were ready, awaiting
his command …

'*Now!*' he hissed, leading the charge from the trees into the open field. There was no hiding the sound of the horses' hooves and the enemy soon spotted them. When they did, Arthur let out a battle cry that was quickly picked up by the others.

Lot's army scrambled, but it was too late. Arthur's men crashed into them. Iron flashed in the moonlight and Excalibur was unstoppable. Even after Arthur had been toppled from his horse and joined others fighting on the ground, it pierced chainmail and breastplates as if they were water. Many of Lot's men had not even had time to put their armour on.

Men fell around Arthur, clutching their wounds, bleeding across the grass. Then a giant rushed at him, sword swinging

wildly. Blocking the blade with his shield,
Arthur brought Excalibur down in an
arc across the man's arm. His opponent
cried out but kept hold of his weapon,
blood seeping through
his sleeve.

He and Arthur circled each other, two beasts sizing up their prey.

Finally they met with a clash that sent Arthur reeling back several steps, tripping over a body. Taking advantage, his opponent pounced, swiping his sword down Arthur's side.

Crying out in pain, Arthur dropped to one knee. His enemy stood over him, sword at his throat.

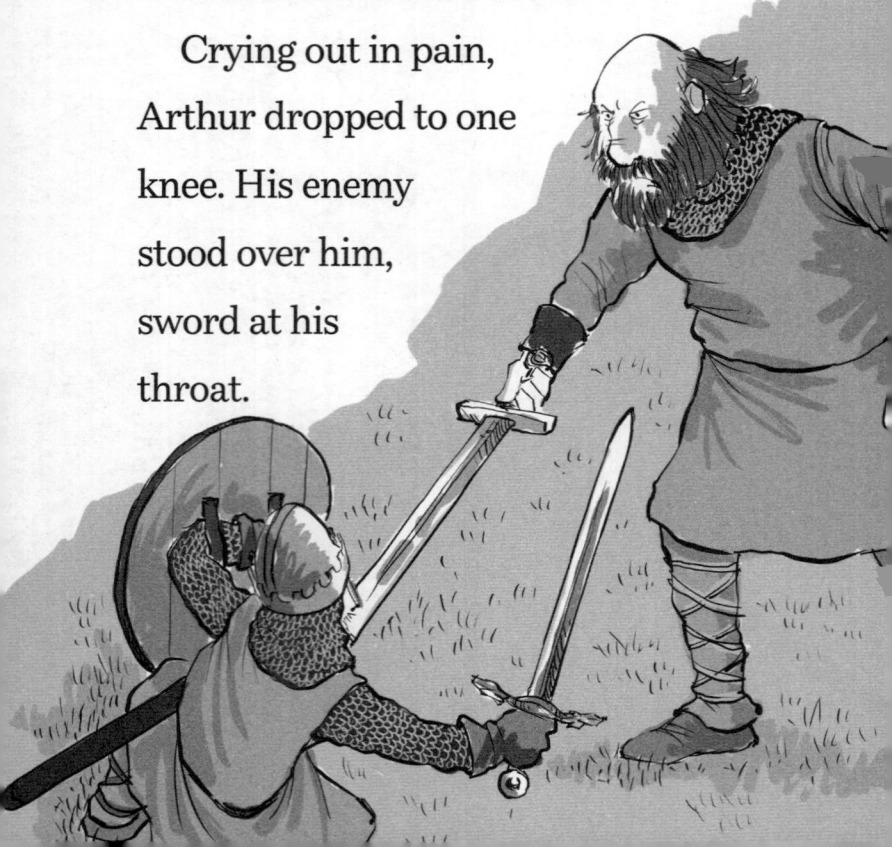

'You will not win this,' the man said. 'Your father may have been a great king, but you are just a boy!'

Arthur grinned, determined not to show fear. '*He* did not pull the sword from the stone. *I* did.' And he rammed his shield upwards into the man's jaw. Leaping to his feet, Arthur made quick work of his dazed opponent, hitting his temple with Excalibur's pommel. The man dropped to the floor, motionless.

Breathing heavily, the world seemed to slow down as Arthur took in the devastation surrounding him. He may have had the element of surprise, but Lot had recovered well. His men were fighting hard, and their sheer numbers were beginning to show. So many of Arthur's men lay dead or injured, that he thought perhaps he should call for a retreat.

Suddenly the air filled with the sound of a war horn. Arthur turned to see his allies King Ban and his brother, Bors, riding to join them. With a renewed sense of hope, Arthur returned to the battle. Surely it would not last long now.

Chapter Four

Four days later, the battle was still raging. Without King Ban's army, Arthur knew he would have been forced to admit defeat already. Many good men

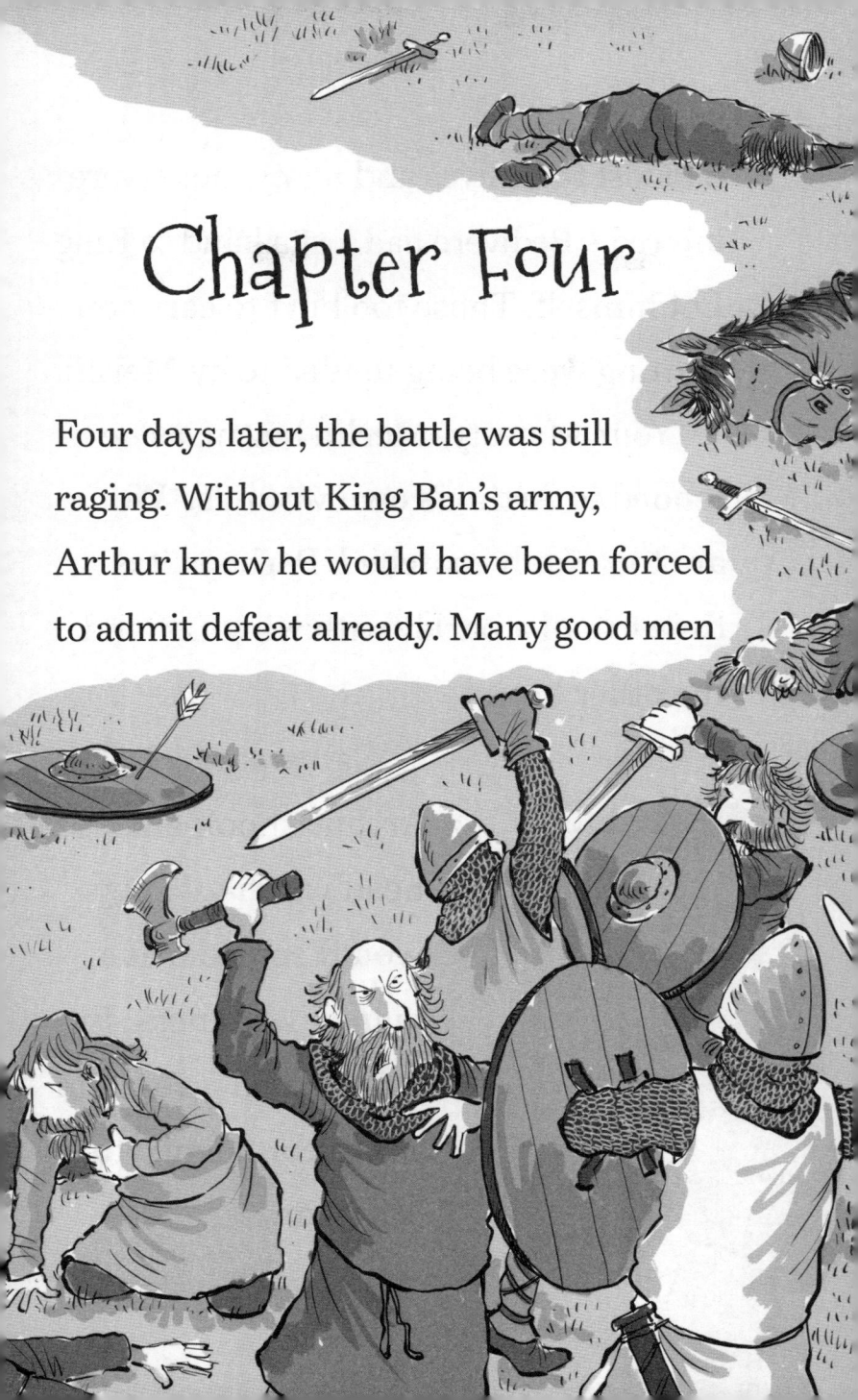

had lost their lives and many more were injured – Bedivere had lost a hand to King Lot himself. Those too hurt to carry on fighting were being tended to by Merlin.

'Your Majesty,' Merlin began, as he tended to Arthur's own wounds. 'We are too evenly matched. Perhaps it is time to call a parley with King Lot and the other kings.'

'Call a parley?' Arthur shook his head wearily. 'They would consider it a sign of weakness. It might even give them more confidence to carry on.'

40

Merlin met his gaze. 'Majesty, they are not stupid men. They know as well as you do that they cannot carry on fighting. They too know that they would be leading many more good men to the slaughter.'

'And if they agree to negotiate, then what? Would you have me agree to their demands? Would you have King Lot rule Britain instead of me?'

'No, Sire. But if you ask them again to accept you as their king, they will.'

Arthur frowned. 'That doesn't sound like Lot.'

'Lot, in particular, is desperate for this war to end. If you give him the choice, he *will* accept, and the others will follow.'

'You're sure of this?'

'I am.'

Arthur knew better than to question how. He pulled on his tunic to leave the tent. 'Then I will send a message. This war ends tonight.'

Llamrei pawed at the ground as Arthur watched King Lot and the ten other kings ride towards him. They were all armed, but none reached for their weapons as they came to a stop before him. Lot was a big man, with wild red hair and a

big bushy beard. A roughly stitched cut
on his forehead still oozed blood and
he looked as weary as Arthur felt.

'You asked to meet with us,' he
stated gruffly, still refusing to use
Arthur's royal title.

Arthur nodded. 'I did. This battle has gone on long enough. If you accept me as the rightful king of Britain, it will end.'

Lot laughed harshly.

'You want me to accept *you* as king? Never!'

'Even if it means continuing to leave your lands undefended because your army is here? What of your other enemies?' It was Merlin who spoke.

Lot glared at him. 'What of them?'

'If you stay here you will be invaded by the Saxons. I have seen it,' Merlin said. 'And I know that you received a letter from you wife Morgause only yesterday begging you to return.'

Hearing his eldest half-sister's name, Arthur glanced at Merlin.

'The Saxons are gathering their forces as we speak,' Merlin continued.

A flicker of fear on Lot's face and the sidelong glances of the other kings told Arthur that Merlin was right.

'Bow to me now and you can return north to defend your lands,' Arthur promised.

'And if we don't?'

'Then you lose everything.'

Lot clenched his jaw. It was the last thing he wanted to hear, but he had no choice. 'So be it,' he announced. Dismounting, he came to kneel before Arthur. The other kings followed. 'Arthur Pendragon, I accept you as the rightful king of this land, and hereby pledge my loyalty as your ally.'

In turn, the other kings repeated these words, begrudgingly bowing their heads and kneeling.

'I accept your allegiance,' Arthur said solemnly. 'Now go. Protect your homes and families. May God be with you.'

Still glaring, Lot climbed back onto his horse. 'Do not think *we* were your only problem,' he warned.

'What do you mean?'

'There is another who would see you destroyed. His name is King Rience.'

'And where is he?'

'Right now he should be riding towards Cameliard.'

Arthur's eyes widened. 'King Leodegrance!' he said to Merlin. Leodegrance had been the first to accept Arthur as High King. He was as loyal to Arthur as he had been to his father, Uther. Cameliard was his home.

Lot continued. 'Rience plans to take as many castles and as much land from you as he can. Then he'll come for you as he has your friends.'

Sensing Arthur's distress, Llamrei tossed her head and reared onto her hind legs.

'If you go now, you may save him,' Lot suggested, snapping his reins. 'But be warned!' he called back, as his forces turned to leave. 'Rience wastes no time when there is war to be had.'

Chapter Five

Arthur breathed a sigh of relief as Cameliard came into view. It was a small castle surrounded by a moat on the border of Wales and Britain. There was no sign of Rience or his forces, but riding across the open plain with a handful of men, Arthur saw two guards crossing the drawbridge to meet him. The guards lowered their spears as he drew near.

'I come in peace!' Arthur cried.

The guards' eyes fell to the Pendragon coat of arms.

'You're ...' the taller man spluttered, before lifting his spear again and dropping to his knee. 'Your Majesty, we are – we are *honoured*.'

'I must speak with King Leodegrance,' Arthur announced, dismounting and handing the reins to Merlin.

The guard stood. 'Of course, Your Majesty. Come this way.'

Arthur followed, Kay at his shoulder, whilst the rest of his knights waited outside. A few moments after entering the receiving room, the door burst open and a middle-aged man entered. He looked pleasantly surprised. 'When Erec told me that King Arthur Pendragon himself had come to see me, I thought he was joking!' he declared, smiling broadly as he made his way over to Arthur.

'I bring grave news,' Arthur began

swiftly. 'King Rience intends to attack Cameliard.'

Leodegrance's smile vanished and his face paled. 'Are you sure?'

'Very sure. I heard it from King Lot himself, and Merlin has seen that he rides towards you as we speak.'

Leodegrance began pacing the floor anxiously. 'My men are few … and from what I hear of Rience – I do not stand a chance, Your Majesty.'

'That is why I am here,' Arthur assured him. 'My forces will set up camp outside

Cameliard. We shall lay in wait, and when Rience comes, we will be ready.'

'I … That is …' Leodegrance looked at Arthur, too grateful to speak further.

Arthur put his hand on the older man's shoulder. 'Say nothing of it, my friend. All I ask is that you lend us what men you can spare.'

Erec, the guardsman from before, stepped forwards. 'Your Majesty, I would be honoured to fight with you.'

Arthur nodded. 'Thank you, Erec. Gather as many fighting men, weapons and horses as you can.'

Bowing, Erec left the room.

'Do you know when Rience and his forces will arrive?' Leodegrance asked.

'Merlin says three days.'

'Then tonight we feast,' Leodegrance announced, forcing his fears aside for the moment.

Arthur entered the Great Hall alongside Lord Leodegrance, Kay and Merlin following behind. He breathed in the smell of roast boar and venison.

The room was filled with music and bursting with men, his own and King Leodegrance's. All were eager to eat, drink and be as merry as they could before the approaching battle.

Servants carried platters of fruit, bread and cheese between benches that ran the length of the hall. Others carried flagons of wine and ale, stopping every now and then to fill up empty cups. Dogs loped from guest to guest, hoping to beg a few scraps.

As Arthur's gaze wandered, he caught sight of the most beautiful woman in the room. She sat alone at the high table, her attention on the dog at her feet as she spoke softly to it. Her dark brown hair fell in waves to her waist, and she wore a dark blue dress.

'Your Majesty, allow me to introduce you to my daughter.' Leodegrance gestured towards the high table.

Arthur's mouth went suddenly dry as he followed his host towards the beautiful woman.

'Guinevere!' Leodegrance cried. 'My dear, I'd like you to meet King Arthur Pendragon.'

Guinevere had stood to embrace her father. Now she smiled up at Arthur and curtsied. 'Good evening, Your Majesty.'

Arthur's heart was pounding. 'Good evening,' he replied, unable to look away. Guinevere blushed.

'Perhaps you would like to sit here,' Leodegrance suggested, indicating the seat beside his daughter.

'With pleasure.'

Leodegrance made his way to his own seat and clapped his hands to summon the attention of his guests. 'We are honoured to have Arthur Pendragon, High King of Britain, here with us today. We do not know what tomorrow will bring, or what may happen when our enemy arrives. But right now we are amongst friends. Right now we feast!'

With that, Leodegrance took the first bite of bread, indicating that the feast had begun. As the room filled again with voices and laughter, Arthur stole a glance at Guinevere. His stomach was so full of nerves, he doubted he would be able to eat anything at all.

Chapter Six

For the next two days, when Arthur wasn't with his men, he was with Guinevere. With each moment he spent with her, he found himself falling more in love. She was as kind as she was beautiful, and she could make him laugh like no one else. Soon he was confiding in her about his fears for the impending war, and his hopes and dreams for the future.

On the last evening before Arthur was to ride out to meet King Rience, Guinevere slipped her arm through his.

'May I speak with you, Sire?' she asked softly.

'Of course.'

'Perhaps we could take a walk outside? The night is warm and the stars are out.'

Arthur smiled. 'I can think of nothing I'd like more.'

As they made their way to the nearest door, he glanced behind and saw that her maid was accompanying them.

For a while, they walked around the courtyard in silence, until Guinevere turned to him. 'Sire, must you fight tomorrow? Are there not others who could take your place?'

Hearing the fear in her voice, Arthur took her hands in his. 'Guinevere, I cannot command others to do what I will not do myself. I am a king.'

'But ... I am afraid,' she whispered, her eyes filling with tears. 'What if I never see you again?'

Arthur wiped the tears as they fell. 'You will,' he promised.

'How can you make such a promise?'

'Because when I return, I intend to ask your father for your hand. If you will have me, that is.'

Guinevere stared at him with eyes that shone even more brilliantly in the moonlight. She had dreamt of hearing him say these words but feared that he would not. 'You wish me to be your wife?'

'More than anything.'

'Oh, Arthur!' she cried joyfully. 'Of course I will have you! How could I say no?'

Happier than he could remember being, Arthur stepped forwards, drawing her hand to his heart. 'And that,' he murmured, kissing her forehead gently, 'is why *nothing* will keep me from returning.'

The following morning, Arthur sat upon Llamrei watching the horizon for any sign of King Rience. He knew his thoughts should be on the battle ahead, but he could not stop thinking about Guinevere.

Finally, they spotted Rience's forces. Rience sat astride a huge warhorse and led the advance, thundering over the plain towards them.

'Stand fast!' Arthur ordered, slipping his visor into place. 'We fight for Britain!'

'*For Britain!*' his men echoed.

Catching sight of Arthur's army, Rience slowed and signalled for his army to do the same.

'Come no further, Rience!' Arthur called out. 'Leave here now or face me in battle!'

Rience laughed. 'You dare to challenge *me*? Boy, I am only too happy to face you. And when I win, I will add your beard to my collection!'

Arthur felt a wave of sickness as Rience turned his horse to show the cloak that draped behind him. It was trimmed with beards of assorted sizes and colours.

'These belonged to the other men who thought they could beat me!'

Arthur could not reason with a madman. He dug his heels into Llamrei's sides. *'For Britain!'* he cried, holding Excalibur aloft. Behind him, men drew their swords and charged.

The two kings found each other quickly: Rience eager for bloodshed, and Arthur keen to avoid it by ending the battle as soon as possible. Their swords clashed and their horses reared. Rience cried out as Excalibur found its

mark and he was flung from his horse, landing awkwardly on the ground.

Arthur dismounted and pushed his way through the fighting with his shield. Rience stood, throwing off the tangle of his cloak. He ignored the blood running down his arm and ran at Arthur, sword raised.

Deflecting the blow, Arthur

moved out of range before darting in for another attack, this time catching Rience squarely on his chainmail shirt. The blow sent Rience reeling backwards. He was almost knocked off his feet as one of Arthur's men crashed into him. Cutting the man down with one swipe, Rience barrelled into Arthur. Both men went crashing to the ground.

A sharp pain tore through Arthur's side. Gritting his teeth, he pushed Rience away, pinning him to the ground as he pressed Excalibur against his throat. Glancing down his body, Arthur saw blood seeping through his shirt from a wound on his side.

That was all the chance Rience needed. Raising his knee, he drove

it into Arthur's stomach, sending
him sprawling. Rolling over, Arthur
staggered to his feet. Summoning
all that was left of his strength, and
thinking only of Guinevere, he charged
repeatedly, swinging Excalibur with all
his might. Rience blocked every blow,
but finally Arthur saw an opening. He
thrust at Rience. Excalibur sank deeply
through metal and flesh.

Rience gasped and fell to the ground.
He looked down at the blade sticking

out of his chest. He looked up at Arthur.
'You–' he gasped, before he slumped
onto the grass and saw no more.

Gazing down at the lifeless body,
Arthur's strength finally left him.

Chapter Seven

Thanks to the protection of the scabbard given to him by the Lady of the Lake, Arthur recovered from his wounds. Because Arthur had fought for Cameliard, Lord Leodegrance was more than happy to grant him his daughter's hand in marriage. Arrangements were made for a wedding to take place at Camelot. It wasn't long before Arthur was well enough to escort Guinevere and her father to her new home.

Their wedding day dawned and Arthur could barely contain his love as Guinevere walked towards him. She carried a small bouquet of pink and blue flowers and wore a crown of the same upon her head. The gown she wore was threaded with gold and finished with a golden band around her waist.

Standing before his bride, his men and God, Arthur couldn't have been prouder to promise himself to her, and he couldn't keep the smile from his face when she made the same promises to him.

Later, during the wedding feast, King Leodegrance called for everyone's attention. The merriment was such that he had to call twice, which only led to more laughter.

'My good friends,' Leodegrance began, grinning and rosy-cheeked

with wine, 'it gives me great pleasure to welcome King Arthur Pendragon into my family. And I have a gift for this great occasion.' He signalled to the guards at a set of side doors, and they opened them to reveal another room.

In the early days, as a farm-boy-turned-boy-king trying to convince older, more experienced men to follow him, Arthur had used the Great Hall to impress. These days he preferred the smaller, plainer meeting room beside it. Now this room was dominated by a large, round table.

Arthur approached it to look more closely, aware of many necks craning behind him to do the same.

'Your Majesty,' Leodegrance explained, 'this table once belonged to your father. Merlin suggested that I have it brought back to Camelot.'

Merlin stepped forwards. 'The Round Table has no head, and therefore no high seat. All men are equal before it,' he said. 'It will be a place for you and your most trusted men to sit and plan. I have given it the power to choose those men most worthy of a place around it.'

'How will we know if we've been chosen?' Kay called out eagerly.

'When you stand before it,

your name will appear written on
the table.'

'What happens when we die?'
someone else called.

'Another man deemed worthy will
take your place.' Merlin looked around
the hall. 'Only one seat
will remain empty: The
Perilous Seat.'

'What's that?' The
question was Bedivere's.

'It is reserved for
the best of men; the
most perfect of you all,'
Merlin explained. 'It
will remain empty until
he comes to Camelot.'

Excited voices filled the air as men began to dream aloud of being chosen. Arthur was honoured by the gift. 'Thank you, my friends. This is a gift like no other. As of tomorrow, I invite any man, be he high-born or low-, to come and stand before the table. Let the word spread far and wide, that Camelot welcomes everyone.'

♦

Word did spread about the Round Table, but the following day it was Arthur's own brother Kay who was first to be chosen to sit at it. Just as Merlin had said it would, Kay's name appeared magically in writing, then Pellinore and Bedivere's. Erec, King Leodegrance's man, was next. He was the first of several from Cameliard to be considered worthy.

Many other men tried and failed, but their disappointment was soothed by the promise that they still had a place at Camelot.

One day, a travel-weary man no older than Arthur entered Camelot. He was a tall man, clearly a strong warrior, who carried himself with pride.

'Your Majesty,' he murmured,

kneeling respectfully. 'I would offer you my services, and my sword.'

The newcomer seemed somehow familiar to Arthur, yet he knew they had not met before. 'What is your name?' he asked.

'Gawain of Lothian, Sire.' The man was careful to avoid eye contact as he answered.

Arthur studied him for a moment.

'Then you are King Lot's son?' *And my half-sister's*, he added silently. *My nephew.*

'I am.'

'Stand, Gawain,' Arthur commanded. 'Your father fought for what he believed in – I cannot hold that against him. How is he?'

'He is well, Your Majesty. He is still in Lothian.'

Arthur nodded. 'And you wish to fight for me?'

'I do.'

'And you are aware that I seek only one more man, besides he who will one day sit in The Perilous Seat?'

'Yes, Sire.'

'Then come with me.'

Arthur led Gawain to the Round Table, where he stood behind one of two empty seats. It took only a moment for Gawain's name to begin appearing, inscribed into the tabletop

by an unseen hand. When it was done, Gawain and Arthur smiled at each other. In years to come, the final seat would be taken too. But for now, the Knights of the Round Table were complete.

CONTINUE THE QUEST WITH THE NEXT BOOK IN THE SERIES!

"This series opens the door to a treasure house of wonderful stories which have previously been available chiefly to older readers. We can only welcome it as a fabulous resource for all who love magical tales, and those who will come to love them."

JOHN MATTHEWS

AUTHOR OF THE RED DRAGON RISING SERIES AND ARTHUR OF ALBION